O Mary, conceived without sin, pray
for those who turn to You. Amen

For N.R.S.M.,
in gratitude for the miracle,
and for Mônica Antunes,
who never squandered her blessings

Daughters of Jerusalem, weep not
for me, but weep for yourselves,
and for your children.

Luke 23:28

Preface and Greeting

In December 1945, two brothers looking for a place to rest found an urn full of papyruses in a cave in the region of Hamra Dom, in Upper Egypt. Instead of telling the local authorities – as the law demanded – they decided to sell them singly in the market for antiquities, thus avoiding attracting the government's attention. The boys' mother, fearing 'negative energies', burned several of the newly discovered papyruses.

The following year, for reasons history does not record, the brothers quarrelled. Attributing this quarrel to those supposed 'negative energies', the mother handed over the manuscripts to a priest, who sold them to the Coptic Museum in Cairo. There, the papyruses were given the name they still bear to this day: Manuscripts from Nag Hammadi (a reference to the town nearest to the caves where they were found). One of the museum's experts, the religious historian Jean Doresse, realised the importance of the discovery and mentioned it for the first time in a publication dated 1948.

Other papyruses began to appear on the black market. The Egyptian government tried to prevent the manuscripts from leaving the country. After the 1952 revolution, most of the material was handed over to the Coptic Museum in Cairo and declared part of the national heritage. Only one text eluded them, and this had turned up in an antiquarian shop in Belgium. After vain attempts to sell it in New York and Paris, it was finally acquired by the Carl Jung Institute in 1951. On the death of the famous psychoanalyst, the papyrus, now known as Jung Codex, returned to Cairo, where the almost one thousand pages and fragments of the Manuscripts from Nag Hammadi are now to be found.

* * *

The papyruses are Greek translations of texts written between the end of the first century BC and AD 180, and they constitute a body of work also known as the Apocryphal Gospels, because they are not included in the Bible as we know it today. Now why is that?

In AD 170, a group of bishops met to decide which texts would form part of the New Testament. The criterion was simple enough: anything that could be used to combat the heresies and doctrinal divisions of the age would be included. The four gospels we know today were chosen, as were the letters from the apostles and whatever else was judged to be, shall we say, 'coherent' with what the bishops believed to be the main tenets of Christianity. Reference to this meeting of the bishops and their list of authorised books can be found in the Muratorian Canon. The other books, like those found in Nag Hammadi, were omitted, either because they were written by women (for example, the Gospel according to Mary Magdalene) or because they depicted a Jesus who was aware of his divine mission and whose passage through death would, therefore, be less drawn out and painful.

* * *

In 1974, the English archaeologist Sir Walter Wilkinson discovered another manuscript, this time written in three languages: Arabic, Hebrew and Latin. Conscious of the laws protecting such finds in the region, he sent the text to the Department of Antiquities in the Museum of Cairo. Shortly afterwards, back came a response: there were at least 155 copies of the document circulating in the world (three of which belonged to the museum) and they were all practically identical. Carbon-14 tests (used to determine the age of organic matter) revealed that the document was relatively recent, possibly as late as 1307. It was easy enough to trace its origin to the city of Accra, outside Egyptian territory. There were, therefore, no restrictions on its removal from the country, and Sir Walter received written permission from the Egyptian government (Ref. 1901/317/IFP-75, dated 23 November 1974) to take it back to England with him.

*   *   *

I met Sir Walter's son in 1982, at Christmas, in Porthmadog in Wales. I remember him mentioning the manuscript discovered by his father, but neither of us gave much importance to the matter. We maintained a cordial relationship over the years and met on at least two other occasions when I visited Wales to promote my books.

On 30 November 2011, I received a copy of the text he had mentioned at that first meeting. I transcribe it here.

I would so like to begin by writing:

**'Now that I am at the end of my life,
I leave for those who come after me
everything that I learned while I walked
the face of this Earth. May they make
good use of it.'**

Alas, that is not true. I am only twenty-one, my parents gave me love and an education, and I married a woman I love and who loves me in return. However, tomorrow, life will undertake to separate us, and we must each set off in search of our own path, our own destiny or our own way of facing death.

As far as our family is concerned, today is the fourteenth of July 1099. For the family of Yakob, the childhood friend with whom I used to play in this city of Jerusalem, it is the year 4859 – he always takes great pride in telling me that Judaism is a far older religion than mine. For the worthy Ibn al-Athir, who spent his life trying to record a history that is now coming to a conclusion, the year 492 is about to end. We do not agree about dates or about the best way to worship God, but in every other respect we live together in peace.

A week ago, our commanders held a meeting. The French soldiers are infinitely superior and far better equipped than ours. We were given a choice: to abandon the city or fight to the death, because we will certainly be defeated. Most of us decided to stay.

The Muslims are, at this moment, gathered at the Al-Aqsa Mosque, while the Jews choose to assemble their soldiers in Mihrab Dawud – the Tower of David – and the Christians, who live in various different quarters, have been charged with defending the southern part of the city.

Outside, we can already see the siege towers built from the enemy's dismantled ships. Judging from the enemy's movements, we assume that they will attack tomorrow morning, spilling our blood in the name of the Pope, the 'liberation' of the city and the 'divine will'.

This evening, in the same square where, a millennium ago, the Roman governor, Pontius Pilate, handed Jesus over to the mob to be crucified, a group of men and women of all ages went to see the Greek, whom we all know as the Copt.

The Copt is a strange man. As an adolescent, he decided to leave his native city of Athens to go in search of money and adventure. He ended up, close to starvation, knocking on the doors of our city, and, when he was well received, he gradually abandoned the idea of continuing his journey and resolved to stay.

He managed to find work in a shoemaker's shop and – just like Ibn al-Athir – he started recording everything he saw and heard for posterity. He did not seek to join any particular religion, and no one tried to persuade him otherwise. As far as he is concerned, we are not in the year 1099 or 4859, much less at the end of 492. The Copt believes only in the present moment and what he calls Moira – the unknown god, the Divine Energy, responsible for a single law, which, if ever broken, will bring about the end of the world.

Alongside the Copt were the patriarchs of the three religions that had settled in Jerusalem. No government official was present during this conversation; they were too preoccupied with making the final preparations for a resistance that we believe will prove utterly pointless.

'Many centuries ago, a man was judged and condemned in this square,' the Greek said. 'On the road to the right, while he was walking towards his death, he passed a group of women. When he saw them weeping, he said: "Weep not for me, weep for Jerusalem." He prophesied what is happening now. From tomorrow, harmony will become discord. Joy will be replaced by grief. Peace will give way to a war that will last into an unimaginably distant future.'

No one said anything, because none of us knew exactly why we were there. Would we have to listen to yet another sermon about these invaders who call themselves 'crusaders'?

For a moment, the Copt appeared to savour the general confusion. And then, after a long silence, he explained:

'They can destroy the city, but they cannot destroy everything the city has taught us, which is why it is vital that this knowledge does not suffer the same fate as our walls, houses and streets. But what is knowledge?'

When no one replied, he went on:

'It isn't the absolute truth about life and death, but the thing that helps us to live and confront the challenges of day-to-day life. It isn't what we learn from books, which serves only to fuel futile arguments about what happened or will happen; it is the knowledge that lives in the hearts of men and women of good will.'

The Copt said:

'I am a learned man and yet, despite having spent all these years restoring antiquities, classifying objects, recording dates and discussing politics, I still don't know quite what to say to you. But I will ask the Divine Energy to purify my heart. You will ask me questions and I will answer them. That is what the teachers of Ancient Greece did; their disciples would ask them questions about problems they had not yet considered, and the teachers would answer them.'

'And what shall we do with your answers?' someone asked.

'Some will write down what I say. Others will remember my words. The important thing is that tonight you will set off for the four corners of the world, telling others what you have heard. That way, the soul of Jerusalem will be preserved. And one day we will be able to rebuild Jerusalem, not just as a city, but as a centre of knowledge and a place where peace will once again reign.'

'We all know what awaits us tomorrow,' said another man. 'Wouldn't it be better to discuss how to negotiate for peace or prepare ourselves for battle?'

The Copt looked at the other religious men beside him and then immediately turned back to the crowd.

'None of us can know what tomorrow will hold, because each day has its good and its bad moments. So, when you ask your questions, forget about the troops outside and the fear inside. Our task is not to leave a record of what happened on this date for those who will inherit the Earth; history will take care of that. We will speak, therefore, about our daily lives, about the difficulties we have had to face. That is all the future will be interested in, because I do not believe very much will change in the next thousand years.'

Then my neighbour Yakob said:

'Speak to us about defeat.'

And he answered:

* * *

Does a leaf, when it falls from the tree in winter, feel defeated by the cold?

The tree says to the leaf: 'That's the cycle of life. You may think you're going to die, but you live on in me. It's thanks to you that I'm alive, because I can breathe. It's also thanks to you that I have felt loved, because I was able to give shade to the weary traveller. Your sap is in my sap; we are one thing.'

Does a man who spent years preparing to climb the highest mountain in the world feel defeated when, on reaching that mountain, he discovers that nature has cloaked the summit in storm clouds? The man says to the mountain: 'You don't want me this time, but the weather will change and, one day, I will make it to the top. Meanwhile, you'll still be here waiting for me.'

Does a young man, rejected by his first love, declare that love does not exist? The young man says to himself: 'I'll find someone better able to understand what I feel. And then I will be happy for the rest of my days.'

In the cycle of nature there is no such thing as victory or defeat: there is only movement.

The winter struggles to reign supreme, but, in the end, it is obliged to accept spring's victory, which brings with it flowers and happiness.

The summer would like to make its warm days last for ever, because it believes that warmth is good for the Earth, but, in the end, it has to accept the arrival of autumn, which will allow the Earth to rest.

The gazelle eats the grass and is devoured by the lion. It isn't a matter of who is the strongest, but God's way of showing us the cycle of death and resurrection.

And within that cycle there are neither winners nor losers, there are only stages that must be gone through. When the human heart understands this, it is free and able to accept difficult times and not be deceived by moments of glory.

Both will pass. One will succeed the other. And the cycle will continue until we liberate ourselves from the flesh and find the Divine Energy.

Therefore, when the fighter is in the arena – whether by his own choice or because unfathomable destiny has placed him there – may his spirit be filled with joy at the prospect of the fight ahead. If he holds on to his dignity and his honour, then, even if he loses the fight, he will never be defeated, because his soul will remain intact.

And he will blame no one for what is happening to him. Ever since he fell in love for the first time and was rejected, he has known that this did not put an end to his ability to love. What is true in love is also true in war.

Losing a battle or losing everything we thought we possessed will bring us moments of sadness, but when those moments pass we will discover the hidden strength that exists in each of us, a strength that will surprise us and increase our self-respect.

We will look around and say to ourselves: 'I survived.' And we will be cheered by our words.

Only those who fail to recognise that inner strength will say 'I lost', and be sad.

Others, even though they are suffering because they were defeated and feel humiliated by the things the winners are saying about them, will allow themselves to shed a few tears, but never succumb to self-pity. They know that this is merely a pause in the fighting and that, for the moment, they are at a disadvantage.

They listen to the beating of their own heart. They're aware of being tense and afraid. They consider their life and discover that, despite the fear, their faith is still alive in their soul, driving them onward.

They try to work out what they did wrong and what they did right. They take advantage of this moment of defeat to rest, heal their wounds, devise new strategies and equip themselves better.

Then the day dawns when a new battle knocks on their door. They are still afraid, but they have to act – either that or remain for ever lying on the ground. They get up and face their opponent, remembering the suffering they have endured and which they no longer wish to endure.

Their previous defeat means that this time they must win, because they don't want to suffer the same pain again.

But if victory is not theirs this time, it will be the next time. And if not the next time, then the time after that. The important thing is to get back on your feet.

Only he who gives up is defeated. Everyone else is victorious.

And the day will come when those difficult moments are merely stories to be told proudly to those who will listen, and they will listen respectfully and learn three important things:

Wait patiently for the right moment to act.

Do not let the next opportunity slip by you.

Take pride in your scars.

Scars are medals branded on the flesh, and your enemies will be frightened by them because they are proof of your long experience of battle. Often this will lead them to seek dialogue and to avoid conflict.

Scars speak more loudly than the sword that caused them.

'Describe the defeated ones,' asked
a merchant, when he saw that the
Copt had finished speaking.

And he answered:

*   *   *

The defeated are those who never fail.

Defeat means that we lose a particular battle or war. Failure does not allow us to go on fighting.

Defeat comes when we fail to get something we very much want. Failure does not allow us to dream. Its motto is: 'Expect nothing and you won't be disappointed.'

Defeat ends when we launch into another battle. Failure has no end: it is a lifetime choice.

Defeat is for those who, despite their fears, live with enthusiasm and faith.

Defeat is for the valiant. Only they will know the honour of losing and the joy of winning.

I am not here to tell you that defeat is part of life: we all know that. Only the defeated know Love. Because it is in the realm of love that we fight our first battles – and generally lose.

I am here to tell you that there are people who have never been defeated.

They are the ones who never fought.

They managed to avoid scars, humiliations, feelings of helplessness, as well as those moments when even warriors doubt the existence of God.

Such people can say with pride: 'I never lost a battle.' On the other hand, they will never be able to say: 'I won a battle.'

Not that they care. They live in a universe in which they believe they are invulnerable; they close their eyes to injustices and to suffering; they feel safe because they do not have to deal with the daily challenges faced by those who risk stepping out beyond their own boundaries.

They have never heard the words 'Goodbye' or 'I've come back. Embrace me with the fervour of someone who, having lost me, has found me again.'

Those who were never defeated seem happy and superior, masters of a truth they never had to lift a finger to achieve. They are always on the side of the strong. They're like hyenas, who only eat the leavings of lions.

They teach their children: 'Don't get involved in conflicts, you'll only lose. Keep your doubts to yourself and you'll never have any problems. If someone attacks you, don't get offended or demean yourself by hitting back. There are more important things in life.'

In the silence of the night, they fight their imaginary battles: their unrealised dreams, the injustices to which they turned a blind eye, the moments of cowardice they managed to conceal from other people – but not from themselves – and the love that crossed their path with a sparkle in its eyes, the love God had intended for them, but which they lacked the courage to embrace.

And they promise themselves: 'Tomorrow will be different.'

But tomorrow comes and the paralysing question surfaces in their mind: 'What if it doesn't work out?'

And so they do nothing.

Woe to those who were never beaten! They will never be winners in this life.

'Tell us about solitude,' said a young woman who had been about to marry the son of one of the richest men in the city but was now obliged to flee.

And he answered:

*   *   *

Without solitude, Love will not stay long by your side.

Because Love needs to rest, so that it can journey through the heavens and reveal itself in other forms.

Without solitude, no plant or animal can survive, no soil can remain productive, no child can learn about life, no artist can create, no work can grow and be transformed.

Solitude is not the absence of Love, but its complement.

Solitude is not the absence of company, but the moment when our soul is free to speak to us and help us decide what to do with our life.

Therefore, blessed are those who do not fear solitude, who are not afraid of their own company, who are not always desperately looking for something to do, something to amuse themselves with, something to judge.

If you are never alone, you cannot know yourself.

And if you do not know yourself, you will begin to fear the void.

But the void does not exist. A vast world lies hidden in our soul, waiting to be discovered. There it is, with all its strength intact, but it is so new and so powerful that we are afraid to acknowledge its existence.

The act of discovering who we are will force us to accept that we can go further than we think. And that frightens us. Best not to take the risk. We can always say: 'I didn't do what I should have done because they wouldn't let me.'

That feels more comfortable. Safer. And, at the same time, it's tantamount to renouncing your own life.

Woe to those who prefer to spend their lives saying: 'I never had any opportunities!'

Because with each day that passes, they will sink deeper into the well of their own limitations, and the time will come when they will lack the strength to climb out and rediscover the bright light shining in through the opening above their head.

But blessed be those who say: 'I'm not brave enough.'

Because they know that it is not someone else's fault. And sooner or later, they will find the necessary faith to confront solitude and its mysteries.

*   *   *

For those who are not frightened by the solitude that reveals all mysteries, everything will have a different taste.

In solitude, they will discover the love that might otherwise have arrived unnoticed. In solitude, they will understand and respect the love that left them.

In solitude, they will be able to decide whether it is worth asking that lost love to come back or if they should simply let it go and set off along a new path.

In solitude, they will learn that saying 'No' does not always show a lack of generosity and that saying 'Yes' is not always a virtue.

And those who are alone in this moment need never be frightened by the words of the devil: 'You're wasting your time.'

Or by the chief demon's even more potent words: 'No one cares about you.'

The Divine Energy is listening to us when we speak to other people, but also when we are still and silent and able to accept solitude as a blessing.

And in that moment, Its light illuminates everything around us and helps us to see that we are necessary, and that our presence on Earth makes an immense difference to Its work.

And when we achieve that harmony, we receive more than we asked for.

*   *   *

For those who feel oppressed by solitude, it is important to remember that at life's most significant moments we are always alone.

Take the child emerging from a woman's womb: it doesn't matter how many people are present, the final decision to live rests with the child.

Take the artist and his work: in order for his work to be really good, he needs to be still and hear only the language of the angels.

Take all of us, when we find ourselves face to face with that Unwanted Visitor, Death: we will all be alone at that most important and most feared moment of our existence.

Just as Love is the divine condition, so solitude is the human condition. And for those who understand the miracle of life, those two states peacefully coexist.

And a boy, who had been chosen as one
of those who was to leave, rent his
garments and said:

'My city thinks I am not good enough
to fight. I am useless.'

And he answered:

*   *   *

Some people say: 'No one loves me.' But even in cases of unrequited love there is always the hope that one day it will be requited.

Others write in their diaries: 'My genius goes unrecognised, my talent unappreciated, my dreams scorned.' But for them, too, there is the hope that, after many struggles, things will change.

Others spend their days knocking at doors, explaining: 'I'm looking for work.' They know that, if they are patient, someone will eventually invite them in.

*   *   *

But there are those who wake each morning with a heavy heart. They are not seekers after love, recognition or work.

They say to themselves: 'I'm useless. I live because I have to survive, but no one, absolutely no one, is interested in what I'm doing.'

Outside, the sun is shining, they are surrounded by their family and they try to keep up the mask of happiness because, in the eyes of others, they have everything they ever dreamed of having. But they are convinced that no one there needs them, either because they are too young and their elders appear to have other concerns, or because they are too old and the younger members of the family seem uninterested in what they have to say.

The poet writes a few lines, then throws them away, thinking: 'Nobody's going to be interested in that.'

The labourer arrives for work and merely repeats the same tasks he did yesterday. He believes that, if he was ever dismissed, no one would even notice his absence.

The young woman making a dress takes enormous pains over every detail, and when she wears it to a celebration she reads the message in other people's eyes: You're no prettier or uglier than any of the other girls. Your dress is just one among millions of dresses all over the world, where, at this very moment, similar celebrations are being held – some in great castles, others in small villages where everyone knows everyone else and passes comments on what the other girls are wearing. But no one commented on what she was wearing, which went unnoticed. It was neither pretty nor ugly; it was just another dress.

Useless.

Younger people realise that the world is full of huge problems that they dream of solving, but no one is interested in their views. 'You don't know what the world is really like,' they are told. 'Listen to your elders and then you'll have a better idea of what to do.'

The older people have gained experience and maturity, they have learned about life's difficulties the hard way, but when the moment comes for them to teach these things no one is interested. 'The world has changed,' they are told. 'You have to keep up to date and listen to the young.'

That feeling of uselessness is no respecter of age and never asks permission, but instead corrodes people's souls, repeating over and over: 'No one is interested in you, you're nothing, the world doesn't need your presence.'

In a desperate attempt to give meaning to life, many turn to religion, because a struggle in the name of a faith is always a justification for some grand action that could transform the world. 'We are doing God's work,' they tell themselves.

And they become devout followers, then evangelists and, finally, fanatics.

They don't understand that religion was created in order to share the mystery and to worship, not to oppress or convert others. The greatest manifestation of the miracle of God is life. Tonight, I will weep for you, O Jerusalem, because that understanding of the Divine Unity is about to disappear for the next one thousand years.

*   *   *

Ask a flower in the field: 'Do you feel useful? After all, you do nothing but produce the same flowers over and over.'

And the flower will answer: 'I am beautiful, and beauty is my reason for living.'

Ask the river: 'Do you feel useful, given that all you do is to keep flowing in the same direction?'

And the river will answer: 'I'm not trying to be useful. I'm trying to be a river.'

Nothing in this world is useless in the eyes of God. Not a leaf from a tree falls, not a hair from your head, not even an insect dies because it was of no use. Everything has a reason to exist.

Even you, the person asking the question. 'I'm useless' is the answer you give yourself.

Soon that answer will poison you and you will die while still alive, even though you still walk, eat, sleep and try to have a little fun whenever possible.

Don't try to be useful. Try to be yourself: that is enough, and that makes all the difference.

Walk neither faster nor slower than your own soul, because it is your soul that will teach you the usefulness of each step you take. Sometimes taking part in a great battle will be the thing that will help to change the course of history. But sometimes you can do that simply by smiling, for no reason, at someone you happen to pass in the street.

Without intending to, you might have saved the life of a complete stranger, who also thought he was useless and might have been ready to kill himself – until a smile gave him new hope and confidence.

* * *

Even if you were to study your own life in detail and re-live each moment that you suffered, sweated and smiled beneath the sun, you would still never know exactly when you had been useful to someone else.

A life is never useless. Each soul that came down to Earth is here for a reason.

The people who really help others are not trying to be useful, but are simply leading a useful life. They rarely give advice, but serve as an example.

Do one thing: live the life you always wanted to live. Avoid criticising others and concentrate on fulfilling your dreams. This may not seem very important to you, but God, who sees all, knows that the example you give is helping Him to improve the world. And each day, He will bestow more blessings upon it.

*   *   *

And when the Unwanted Visitor arrives, you will hear it say:

'It is fair to ask: "Father, Father, why hast thou forsaken me?" But now, in this final second of your life on Earth, I am going to tell you what I saw: I found the house clean, the table laid, the fields ploughed, the flowers smiling. I found each thing in its proper place, precisely as it should be. You understood that small things are responsible for great changes. And for that reason, I will carry you up to Paradise.'

**And a woman called Almira,
a seamstress, said:**

**'I could have left before the crusaders
arrived, and if I had, I would now be
working in Egypt, but I was always
too afraid to change.'**

And he answered:

*   *   *

We are afraid to change because we think that, after so much effort and sacrifice, we know our present world.

And even though that world might not be the best of all worlds, and even though we may not be entirely satisfied with it, at least it won't give us any nasty surprises. We won't go wrong.

When necessary, we will make a few minor adjustments so that everything continues the same.

We see that the mountains always stay in the same place. We see that fully grown trees, when transplanted, usually die.

And we say: 'We want to be like the mountains and the trees. Solid and respectable.' Even though, during the night, we wake up thinking: 'I wish I was like the birds, who can visit Damascus and Baghdad and come back whenever they want to.'

Or: 'I wish I was like the wind, for no one knows where it comes from nor where it goes, and it can change direction without ever having to explain why.'

The next day, however, we remember that the birds are always fleeing from hunters and from larger birds; and that the wind sometimes gets caught up in a whirlwind and destroys everything around it.

It's nice to dream that we will have plenty of time in the future to do our travelling and that, one day, we will travel. It cheers us up because we know that we are capable of doing more than we do. Dreaming carries no risks. The dangerous thing is trying to transform your dreams into reality.

But the day will come when Fate knocks on our door. It might be the gentle tapping of the Angel of Good Fortune or the unmistakable rat-a-tat-tat of the Unwanted Visitor. They both say: 'Change now!' Not next week, not next month, not next year. The angels say: 'Now!'

We always listen to the Unwanted Visitor. And we change everything because he scares us: we change village, habits, shoes, food, behaviour. We can't convince the Unwanted Visitor to allow us to stay as we are. There is no discussion.

We also listen to the Angel of Good Fortune, but we ask him: 'Where will this lead?' 'To a new life,' comes the answer.

And we think: 'We have a few problems in our life, but nothing that can't be solved in time. We must serve as an example to our parents, our teachers, our children, and keep to the correct path. Our neighbours expect us to teach everyone the virtue of perseverance, to struggle against adversity and overcome obstacles.'

And we feel proud of ourselves. And we are praised because we refuse to change, continuing, instead, in the direction Fate has chosen for us.

Wrong.

The correct path is the path of nature, which is constantly changing, like the dunes in the desert.

Those who think that the mountains don't change are wrong: they are born out of earthquakes, are eroded by wind and rain, and each day they are slightly different, even though we do not notice.

The mountains change and are pleased: 'It's good not to be the same all the time,' they say to each other.

Those who think the trees don't change are wrong. They have to accept that they will be bare in winter and clothed in summer. And they reach beyond the place where they were planted, because the birds and the wind scatter their seeds.

The trees are glad. 'I thought I was just one tree and now I see that I am many,' they say to their children springing up around them.

*   *   *

Nature is telling us: 'Change!'

And those who do not fear the Angel of Good Fortune understand that they must go forward, despite their fear. Despite their doubts. Despite recriminations. Despite threats.

They confront their values and prejudices. They hear the advice of their loved ones, who say: 'Why do that? You have everything you need: the love of your parents, wife and children, the craft it took you so long to learn. Don't run the risk of becoming a stranger in a strange land.'

Nevertheless, they risk taking a first step – sometimes out of curiosity, sometimes out of ambition – but generally because they feel an uncontrollable longing for adventure.

At each bend in the road, they feel more and more afraid, and yet, at the same time, they surprise themselves: they are stronger and happier.

Joy. That is one of the main blessings of the All-Powerful. If we are happy, we are on the right road.

Fear gradually ebbs away, because it wasn't given what it felt was its due importance.

One question persists as we take our first steps along the path: 'Will my decision to change make other people suffer?'

But if you love someone, then you want your beloved to be happy. You might feel frightened for him initially, but that feeling soon gives way to pride at seeing him doing what he wants to do and going where he always dreamed of going.

Later, we might begin to experience a sense of abandonment and helplessness.

But travellers meet other people on the road who are feeling just the same. As they talk, they realise that they are not alone; they become travelling companions and share their solutions to various obstacles. And they all feel wiser and more alive than they thought they were.

When they are lying in their tents, unable to sleep and overwhelmed by sadness and regret, they say to themselves: 'Tomorrow, and only tomorrow, will I take another step. Besides, I can always turn back, because I know the road, but one more step won't make much difference.'

*   *   *

Until one day, without warning, the road stops testing the traveller and begins to treat him generously. The traveller's troubled spirit takes pleasure in the beauties and the challenges of the new landscape.

And each step, which had until then been merely automatic, becomes instead a conscious step.

Rather than speaking to him of the solace of security, it teaches him the joy of facing new challenges.

The traveller continues his journey. He doesn't complain of boredom now; he complains, rather, that he is tired. But at that point, he rests, enjoys the landscape and then carries on.

Instead of spending his whole life destroying the roads he was afraid of following, he begins to love the road he is on.

Even if his final destination remains a mystery. Even if, at some point, he makes a wrong decision. God sees his courage and sends him the necessary inspiration to put matters right.

What continues to trouble him is not what happens, but a fear that he won't know how to deal with it. Once he has decided to follow his path and has no alternative, he discovers that he has great will power and that events bend to his decisions.

'Difficulty' is the name of an ancient tool that was created purely to help us define who we are.

Religions teach that faith and transformation are the only ways of drawing near to God.

Faith shows us that we are never alone.

Transformation helps us to love the mystery.

And when everything seems dark, and we feel alone and helpless, we won't look back, for fear of seeing the changes that have taken place in our soul. We will look ahead.

We will not fear what happens tomorrow, because yesterday we had someone watching over us.

And that same Presence will remain at our side.

That Presence will shelter us from suffering or give us the strength to face it with dignity.

We will go further than we think. We will seek out the place where the morning star is born. And we will be surprised when we get there how much easier it was than we had imagined.

*   *   *

The Unwanted Visitor visits those who don't change and those who do. But those who did change can say: 'My life was an interesting one. I didn't squander my blessing.'

And to those who believe that adventures are dangerous I say, Try routine: that kills you far more quickly.

And someone said:

'When everything looks black, we need to raise our spirits. So, talk to us about beauty.'

And he answered:

* * *

People always say: 'It's inner beauty that matters, not outer beauty.'
Well, that's not true.
If it were, why would flowers put so much energy into attracting bees? And why would raindrops transform themselves into a rainbow when they encounter the sun? Because nature longs for beauty, and is only satisfied when beauty can be exalted. Outer beauty is inner beauty made visible, and it manifests itself in the light that flows from our eyes. It doesn't matter if a person is badly dressed or doesn't

conform to our idea of elegance, or doesn't
even care about impressing other people. The
eyes are the mirror of the soul and reflect everything that seems to be hidden; and, like a
mirror, they also reflect the person looking into
them. So if the person looking into someone's
eyes has a dark soul, he will see only his own
ugliness.

*   *   *

Beauty is present in all creation, but the dangerous fact is that, because we human beings are
often cut off from the Divine Energy, we allow
ourselves to be influenced by what other people
think. We deny our own beauty because others
can't or won't recognise it. Instead of accepting
ourselves as we are, we try to imitate what we
see around us. We try to be what other people
think of as 'pretty' and, little by little, our soul
fades, our will weakens, and all the potential we
had to make the world a more beautiful place
withers away.

We forget that the world is what we imagine
it to be.

We stop being the moonlight and become, instead, the pool of water reflecting it. Tomorrow, the water will evaporate in the sun. And all because, one day, someone said: 'You are ugly.' Or: 'She is pretty.' With those three simple words, they stole away all our self-confidence.

And we become ugly and embittered.

* * *

At that moment, we can draw comfort from so-called 'wisdom', an accumulation of ideas put together by people wishing to define the world, instead of respecting the mystery of life. This 'wisdom' consists of all the unnecessary rules, regulations and measurements intended to establish a standard of behaviour.

According to that false wisdom, we should not be concerned about beauty because it is superficial and ephemeral.

That isn't true. All the beings created under the sun, from birds to mountains, from flowers to rivers, reflect the miracle of creation.

If we resist the temptation to allow other people to define who we are, then we will gradually be able to let the sun inside our own soul shine forth.

Love passes by and says: 'I never noticed you before.'

And our soul responds: 'Well, pay more attention, because here I am. It took a breeze to blow the dust from your eyes, but now that you have recognised me, don't leave me again, because all of us desire beauty.'

Beauty exists not in sameness but in difference. Who could imagine a giraffe without its long neck or a cactus without its spines? The irregularity of the mountain peaks that surround us is what makes them so imposing. If we tried to make them all the same, they would no longer command our respect.

It is the imperfect that astonishes and attracts us.

When we look at a cedar tree, we don't think: 'The branches should be all the same length.' We think: 'How strong it is.'

When we see a snake, we never say: 'He is crawling along the ground, while I am walking with head erect.' We think: 'He might be small, but his skin is colourful, his movements elegant, and he is more powerful than me.'

When the camel crosses the desert and takes us to the place we want to reach, we never say: 'He's humpbacked and has ugly teeth.' We think: 'He deserves my love for his loyalty and help. Without him, I would never be able to explore the world.'

A sunset is always more beautiful when it is covered with irregularly shaped clouds, because only then can it reflect the many colours out of which dreams and poetry are made.

Pity those who think: 'I am not beautiful. That's why Love has not knocked at my door.' In fact, Love did knock, but when they opened the door they weren't prepared to welcome Love in.

They were too busy trying to make themselves beautiful first, when, in fact, they were fine as they were.

They were trying to imitate others, when Love was looking for something original.

They were trying to reflect what came from outside, forgetting that the brightest light comes from within.

And a young man who would have
to leave that night said:

'I was never sure which direction
to take.'

And he answered:

*   *   *

Like the sun, life spreads its light in all directions.

When we are born, we want everything at once and cannot control the energy we have been given.

But, if we want to make a fire, we have to focus all the sun's rays on one spot.

And the great secret that the Divine Energy revealed to the world was fire. Not just fire for burning, but the fire that transforms wheat into bread.

And there comes a moment when we need to focus that inner fire so that our life will have some meaning.

Then we ask the heavens: 'But what meaning?'

Some immediately brush this question aside: it's bothersome, it won't let you sleep and there's no easy answer. They are the ones who, later on, will live tomorrow as if it were yesterday.

And when the Unwanted Visitor arrives, they will say: 'My life was too short, I squandered my blessing.'

*   *   *

Others embrace the question, but since they don't know the answer they start to read what was written by those who have already faced up to the challenge. And suddenly, they find an answer which they judge to be correct.

When that happens, they become the slaves of that answer. They draw up laws intended to force others to accept what they believe to be the sole reason for existence. They build temples to justify it and courts for those who reject what they consider to be the absolute truth.

*   *   *

Finally, there are those who saw at once that the question was a trap: there is no answer.

Instead of wasting time grappling with that trap, they decide to act. They go back to their childhood and look for what filled them with enthusiasm then and – disregarding the advice of their elders – devote their life to it.

Because Enthusiasm is the Sacred Fire.

They slowly discover that their actions are linked to a mysterious impulse beyond human knowledge. And they bow their head as a sign of respect for that mystery and pray that they will not be diverted from a path they do not know, a path they have chosen to travel because of the flame burning in their hearts.

They use their intuition when they can and resort to discipline when intuition fails them.

They seem quite mad. And sometimes they behave like mad people. But they are not mad. They have discovered true Love and Will.

And those two things reveal the goal and the direction that they should follow.

Their will is crystalline, their love pure and their steps determined. In moments of doubt or sadness, they never forget: 'I am an instrument. Allow me to be an instrument capable of manifesting Your Will.'

They have chosen their road, and they may only understand what their goal is when they find themselves before the Unwanted Visitor. That is the beauty of the person who continues onward with enthusiasm and respect for the mystery of life as his only guide: his road is beautiful and his burden light.

The goal can be large or small, it can be far away or right next door, but he goes in search of it with respect and honour. He knows what each step means and how much it cost in effort, training and intuition.

He focuses not just on the goal to be reached, but on everything happening around him. He often has to stop because his strength fails him.

At such moments, Love appears and says: 'You think you're heading towards a specific point, but the whole justification for the goal's existence lies in your love for it. Rest a little, but as soon as you can, get up and carry on. Because ever since your goal found out that you were travelling towards it, it has been running to meet you.'

*   *   *

Those who ignore the question, those who answer it and those who understand that the only way to confront it is to take action will all meet the same obstacles and be made happy by the same things. But only the person who accepts God's plan with humility and courage knows that he is on the right road.

And a woman who was getting on
in years and had never found a
husband, said:

'Love has always passed me by.'

And he answered:

*　*　*

In order to hear Love's words, you must allow Love to approach.

However, when it does draw near, we fear what it might say to us, because Love is free and is not ruled by our will or by what we do.

All lovers know this, but refuse to accept it. They think they can seduce Love through submission, power, beauty, wealth, tears and smiles.

True Love, however, is the love that seduces and will never allow itself to be seduced.

Love transforms, love heals. But sometimes it lays deadly traps and ends up destroying the person who decided to surrender himself completely. How can the force that moves the world and keeps the stars in their places be, at once, so creative and so devastating?

We are used to thinking that what we give is the same as what we receive, but people who love, expecting to be loved in return, are wasting their time.

Love is an act of faith, not an exchange.

Contradictions are what make love grow. Conflicts are what allow love to remain by our side.

Life is too short for us to keep important words, for example, 'I love you', locked in our hearts.

But do not always expect to hear the same words back. We love because we need to love. Otherwise, love loses all meaning and the sun ceases to shine.

A rose dreams of enjoying the company of bees, but none appears. The sun asks:

'Aren't you tired of waiting?'

'Yes,' answers the rose, 'but if I close my petals I will wither and die.'

And yet, even when Love does not appear, we remain open to its presence. Sometimes, when loneliness seems about to crush everything, the only way to resist is to keep on loving.

*   *   *

Our great goal in life is to love. The rest is silence.

We need to love. Even when it leads us to the land where the lakes are made of tears – that secret, mysterious place, the land of tears!

Tears speak for themselves. And when we feel that we have cried all we needed to cry, they still continue to flow. And just when we believe that our life is destined to be a long walk through the Vale of Sorrows, the tears suddenly vanish.

Because we managed to keep our heart open, despite the pain.

Because we realised that the person who left us did not take the sun with them or leave darkness in their place. They simply left, and with every farewell comes a hidden hope.

It is better to have loved and lost than never to have loved at all.

* * *

Our one true choice is to plunge into the mystery of that uncontrollable force. We could say: 'I've suffered greatly before and I know that this won't last either,' and thus drive Love from our door, but if we did that we would become dead to life.

Because Nature is a manifestation of the Love of God. Regardless of what we do, Nature continues to love us. Let us, therefore, respect and understand what Nature teaches us.

We love because Love sets us free, and we say things that we once never even had the courage to whisper to ourselves.

We make a decision that we kept putting off.

We learn to say 'No' without thinking of that word as somehow cursed.

We learn to say 'Yes' without fearing the consequences.

We forget everything we were taught about Love, because each encounter is different and brings its own agonies and ecstasies.

We sing more loudly when the person we love is far away and whisper poems when he is near, even if he doesn't listen and pays no attention to either our songs or our whispers.

We don't close our eyes to the Universe and then complain: 'It's dark.' We keep our eyes wide open, knowing that the light could lead us to do undreamed-of things. That is all part of love.

Our heart is open to love and we surrender to it without fear, because we have nothing more to lose.

Then when we go home, we find that someone was there waiting for us, looking for the same thing we were looking for and experiencing the same anxieties and longings.

Because love is like the water that is transformed into a cloud: it's lifted up into the heavens, where it can see everything from a distance, aware that, one day, it will have to return to Earth.

Because love is like the cloud that is transformed into rain: it is drawn down to the Earth, where it waters the fields.

Love is only a word, until we decide to let it possess us with all its force.

Love is only a word, until someone arrives to give it meaning.

Don't give up. Remember, it's always the last key on the key ring that opens the door.

However, one young man disagreed:

'Your words are beautiful, but the truth
is that we never have much choice. Life
and our community have already taken
charge of planning our fate.'

An old man added:

'And I can't go back and recover
lost moments.'

And he answered:

*   *   *

What I am about to say may be of no use on the eve of an invasion. Nevertheless, take note of my words so that, one day, everyone may know how we lived in Jerusalem.

*   *   *

After thinking a little, the Copt went on:

*   *   *

No one can go back, but everyone can go forward.

And tomorrow, when the sun rises, all you have to say to yourselves is:

I am going to think of this day as the first day of my life.

I will look on the members of my family with surprise and amazement, glad to discover that they are by my side, silently sharing that much-talked-about but little understood thing called love.

I will ask to join the first camel train that appears on the horizon, without asking where it is going. And I will leave it as soon as something more interesting catches my eye.

I will pass a beggar, who will ask me for money. I might give it to him or I might walk past thinking that he will only spend it on drink, and as I do I will hear his insults and know that it is simply his way of communicating with me.

I will pass someone trying to destroy a bridge. I might try to stop him or I might realise that he is doing it because he has no one waiting for him on the other side. This is his way of trying to fend off his own loneliness.

I will look at everything and everyone as if for the first time, especially the small things that I have grown used to, quite forgetting the magic surrounding them. The desert sands, for example, which are moved by an energy I cannot understand – because I cannot see the wind.

Instead of noting down things I'm unlikely to forget on the piece of parchment I always carry with me, I will write a poem. Even if I have never written one before and even if I never do so again, I will at least know that I once had the courage to put my feelings into words.

When I reach a small village that I know well, I will enter it by a different route. I will be smiling, and the inhabitants will say to each other: 'He must be mad, because war and destruction have left the soil barren.'

But I will keep smiling, because it pleases me to know that they think I am mad. My smile is my way of saying: 'You can destroy my body, but not my soul.'

Tonight, before leaving, I'm going to spend time sorting through the pile of things I never had the patience to put in order. And I will find that a little of my history is there. All the letters, the notes, the cuttings and receipts will take on their own life and have strange stories to tell me – about the past and about the future. All the different things in the world, all the roads travelled, all the entrances and exits of my life.

I am going to put on a shirt I often wear and, for the first time, I am going to notice how it was made. I am going to imagine the hands that wove the cotton and the river where the fibres of the plant were born. I will understand that all those now invisible things are a part of the history of my shirt.

And even the things I am accustomed to – like the sandals which, after long use, have become an extension of my feet – will be clothed in the mystery of discovery.

Since I am heading off into the future, I will be helped by the scuff marks left on my sandals from when I stumbled in the past.

May everything my hand touches and my eyes see and my mouth tastes be different, but the same. That way, all those things will cease to be still and instead will explain to me why they have been with me for such a long time; and they will reveal to me the miracle of re-encountering emotions worn smooth by routine.

I will drink some tea that I have never tried before because others told me it tasted horrible. I will walk down a street I have never walked down before because others told me it was totally without interest. And I will find out whether or not I would like to go back there.

If it's sunny tomorrow, I want to look at the sun properly for the first time.

If it's cloudy, I want to watch to see in which direction the clouds are going. I always think that I don't have time or that I don't pay enough attention. Tomorrow, though, I will concentrate on the direction taken by the clouds, or on the sun's rays and the shadows they create.

Above my head exists a sky about which all humanity, over thousands of years, has woven a series of reasonable explanations.

Well, I will forget everything I learned about the stars and they will be transformed once more into angels or children or whatever I feel like believing at that moment.

Time and life have given me plenty of logical explanations for everything, but my soul feeds on mysteries. I need mystery. I need to see the voice of an angry god in a rumble of thunder, even though many of you here might consider that heresy.

I want to fill my life with fantasy again, because an angry god is far stranger, far more frightening and far more interesting than a phenomenon explained by the sages.

For the first time, I will smile without feeling guilty, because joy is not a sin.

For the first time, I will avoid anything that makes me suffer, because suffering is not a virtue.

I will not complain about life, saying: 'Everything's always the same and I can do nothing to change it.' Because I am living this day as if it were my first and, while it lasts, I will discover things that I did not even know were there.

Even though I have walked past the same places countless times before and said 'Good morning' to the same people, this day's 'Good morning' will be different. It will not be a mere polite formula, it will be a form of blessing, in the hope that everyone I speak to will understand the importance of being alive, even when tragedy is threatening to engulf us.

I will pay attention to the words of the song the minstrel is singing in the street, even though others are not listening because their souls are heavy with fear. The music says: 'Love rules, but no one knows where it has its throne; in order to know that secret place, you must first submit to Love.'

And I will have the courage to open the door to the sanctuary that leads to my soul.

May I look at myself as if this were the first time I had ever been in contact with my own body and my own soul.

May I be capable of accepting myself as I am: a person who walks and feels and talks like anyone else, but who, despite his faults, is also brave.

May I be amazed by my simplest gestures, as though I were talking to a stranger; by my most ordinary emotions, as though I were feeling the sand stinging my face when the wind blows in from Baghdad; by the most tender of moments, as when I watch my wife sleeping by my side and try to imagine what she is dreaming.

And if I'm alone in bed, I will go over to the window, look up at the sky and feel certain that loneliness is a lie, because the Universe is there to keep me company.

And then I will have lived each hour of my day as if it were a constant surprise to me, to this 'I', who was not created by my father or my mother or by school, but by everything I have experienced up until now, and which I suddenly forgot in order to discover it all anew.

And even if this is to be my last day on Earth, I will enjoy it to the full, because I will live it with the innocence of a child, as if I were doing everything for the first time.

And the wife of a trader said:

'Speak to us about sex.'

And he answered:

*   *   *

Men and women whisper to each other because they have turned a sacred gesture into a sinful act.

This is the world in which we live. And while robbing the present moment of its reality can be dangerous, disobedience can also be a virtue, when we know how to use it.

If two bodies merely join together, that is not sex, it is merely pleasure. Sex goes far beyond pleasure.

In sex, relaxation and tension go hand in hand, as do pain and pleasure and shyness and the courage to go beyond one's limits.

How can such opposing states exist in harmony together? There is only one way: by surrendering yourself.

Because the act of surrender means: 'I trust you.'

It isn't enough to imagine everything that might happen if we allowed ourselves to join not just our bodies, but our souls as well.

Let us plunge together, then, down the dangerous path of surrender. It may be dangerous, but it is the only path worth following.

And even if this causes major changes in our world, we have nothing to lose, because by opening the door that unites body and soul, what we gain is total love.

Let us forget all that we are taught about how it is noble to give and humiliating to receive. For most people, generosity consists only in giving, and yet receiving is also an act of love. Allowing someone else to make us happy will make them happy too.

*   *   *

When we are too generous in the sexual act and our main preoccupation is with our partner's pleasure, our own pleasure can be diminished or even destroyed.

When we are capable of giving and receiving with the same intensity, our body becomes as tense as the string on a bow, but our mind relaxes like the arrow about to be fired. Our brain is no longer in charge; instinct is our only guide.

When body and soul meet and the Divine Energy fills not only those parts that most people consider to be erotic, but also every hair and every inch of skin, they give off a light of a different colour. Two rivers meet to become a more beautiful, more powerful river.

Everything that is spiritual manifests itself in visible form, and everything that is visible is transformed into spiritual energy.

Everything is permitted, if everything is accepted.

Sometimes love grows tired of speaking softly. Therefore, let it reveal itself in all its splendour, burning like the sun and destroying whole forests with its winds.

If one of the lovers surrenders completely, then the other will do the same, because embarrassment will have become curiosity, and curiosity leads us to explore all the things we did not know about ourselves.

See sex as a gift, a ritual of transformation. And as in any ritual, ecstasy will be present to glorify the end, but it is not the sole objective. What matters is that we have travelled a road with our partner that led us into unknown territory, where we encountered gold and incense and myrrh.

Give the sacred its full sacred meaning. And should moments of doubt arise, always remember: we are not alone at such moments; both parties are feeling the same thing.

Fearlessly open the secret box of your fantasies. One person's courage will help the other person to be equally brave.

True lovers will be able to enter the garden of beauty without fear of being judged. They will no longer be two bodies and two souls meeting, but a single fountain out of which pours the true water of life.

The stars will contemplate the lovers' naked bodies, and the lovers will feel no shame. The birds will fly close by, and the lovers will imitate the songs of the birds. Wild animals will approach cautiously, because what they are seeing is far wilder than they are. And they will bow their heads as a sign of respect and submission.

And time will cease to exist, because in the land of pleasure-born-of-true-love, everything is infinite.

And one of the combatants who was preparing to die the next day, but who, nonetheless, had chosen to come to the square to hear what the Copt had to say, commented:

'We were divided when what we wanted was unity. The cities that lay in the path of the invaders suffered the consequences of a war they did not choose. What should the survivors tell their children?'

And he answered:

*   *   *

We were born alone and we will die alone. But, while we are on this planet, we must accept and glorify our act of faith through other people.

Community is life: from it comes our capacity for survival. That is how it was when we lived in caves, and so it is today.

Respect those who grew up and learned alongside you. Respect those who taught you. When the day comes, tell your stories and teach; that way the community can continue to exist and our traditions remain unchanged.

Anyone who does not share his moments of joy and discouragement with others will never fully know his own qualities and his own defects.

*　*　*

Meanwhile, be alert to a danger that threatens all communities: people being drawn into a standard way of behaving, taking as their model their own limitations, fears and prejudices.

That is a very high price to pay, because in order for you to be accepted you will have to please everyone.

And that is not proof of love for the community, but proof of a lack of love for oneself.

You will only be loved and respected if you love and respect yourself. Never try to please everyone; if you do, you will be respected by no one.

Seek friends and allies among people who believe in what they are doing and in who they are.

I'm not saying: 'Seek out people who think the same as you.' I'm saying: 'Seek out those who think differently from you and whom you will never be able to convince that you are right.'

Because friendship is one of the many faces of Love, and Love is not swayed by opinions; Love accepts its companion unconditionally and allows each to grow in his or her own way.

Love is an act of faith in another person, not an act of surrender.

Do not seek to be loved at any price, because Love has no price.

Your friends are not the kind who attract everyone's gaze, who dazzle, and say: 'There is no one better, more generous or more virtuous in the whole of Jerusalem.'

Your friends are the sort who do not wait for things to happen in order to decide which attitude to take; they decide on the spur of the moment, even though they know it could be risky.

They are free spirits who can change direction whenever life requires them to. They explore new paths, recount their adventures, and thus enrich both city and village.

If they once took a wrong and dangerous path, they will never come to you and say: 'Don't ever do that.'

They will merely say: 'I once took a wrong and dangerous path.'

This is because they respect your freedom, just as you respect theirs.

Avoid at all costs those who are only by your side in moments of sadness to offer consoling words. What they are actually saying to themselves is: 'I am stronger. I am wiser. I would not have taken that step.'

Stay close to those who are by your side in happy times, because they do not harbour jealousy or envy in their hearts, only joy to see you happy.

Avoid those who believe they are stronger than you, because they are actually concealing their own fragility.

Stay close to those who are not afraid to be vulnerable, because they have confidence in themselves and know that, at some point in our lives, we all stumble; they do not interpret this as a sign of weakness, but of humanity.

Avoid those who talk a great deal before acting, those who never take a step without being quite sure that it will bring them respect.

Stay close to those who, when you made a mistake, never said: 'I would have done it differently.' They did not make that particular mistake and so are in no position to judge.

Avoid those who seek friends in order to maintain a certain social status or to open doors they would not otherwise be able to approach.

Stay close to those who are only interested in opening one important door – the door to your heart. For they will never invade your soul without your consent, or shoot a deadly arrow through that open door.

Friendship is like a river: it flows around rocks, adapts itself to valleys and mountains, occasionally turns into a pool until the hollow in the ground is full and it can continue on its way.

Just as the river never forgets that its goal is the sea, so friendship never forgets that its only reason for existing is to love other people.

Avoid those who say: 'That's it, I'll go no further.' Because what they have failed to grasp is that neither life nor death has an end; they are merely stages of eternity.

Stay close to those who say: 'Everything's fine as it is, but we still need to move on.' Because they understand the need to keep going beyond the known horizon.

Avoid those who meet up to discuss, seriously and pretentiously, any decisions that the community needs to take. They understand politics; they impress others and try to show how wise they are. What they don't understand is that it is impossible to control so much as the fall of a single hair on your head. Discipline is important, but it needs to leave doors and windows open to intuition and the unexpected.

Stay close to those who sing, tell stories and enjoy life, and whose eyes sparkle with happiness. Because happiness is contagious and will always manage to find a solution, whereas logic can find only an explanation for the mistake made.

Stay close to those who allow the light of Love to shine forth without restrictions, judgements or rewards, without letting it be blocked by the fear of being misunderstood.

No matter how you are feeling, get up every morning and prepare to let your light shine forth.

Those with eyes to see will see your light and be enchanted by it.

A young woman who rarely left her
house because she thought no one was
interested in her said:

'Teach us about elegance.'

Everyone in the courtyard muttered,
'What kind of question is that to ask
when we are about to be invaded, when
blood will soon be running down every
street in the city?'

However, the Copt smiled, and his smile
was not a mocking one but filled
with respect for the young woman's
courage.

And he answered:

*   *   *

Elegance tends to be mistaken for superficiality and mere appearance. Nothing could be further from the truth: some words are elegant, some can wound and destroy, but all are written with the same letters. Flowers are elegant, even when hidden among the grasses in a meadow. The gazelle when it runs is elegant, even when it is fleeing from a lion.

Elegance is not an outer quality, but a part of the soul that is visible to others.

And even when passions run high, elegance does not allow the real ties binding two people to be broken.

Elegance lies not in the clothes we wear, but in the way we wear them.

It isn't in the way we wield a sword, but in the dialogue we hold that could avoid a war.

* * *

Elegance is achieved when, having discarded all superfluous things, we discover simplicity and concentration. The simpler the pose, the better; the more sober, the more beautiful.

And what is simplicity? It is the coming together of the true values of life.

Snow is pretty because it has only one colour.

The sea is pretty because it appears to be a flat plane.

The desert is beautiful because it seems to consist only of sand and rocks.

However, when we look more closely at each of these things, we discover how profound and complete they are, and recognise their qualities.

The simplest things in life are the most extraordinary. Let them reveal themselves.

Consider the lilies of the field, how they grow; they neither toil nor spin. And yet even Solomon in all his glory was not arrayed like one of these.

The nearer the heart comes to simplicity, the more capable it is of loving freely and without fear. The more fearlessly it loves, the more capable it is of revealing elegance in its every gesture.

Elegance is not a matter of good taste. Every culture has its own idea of beauty, which is often completely different from ours.

But every tribe, every people, has values that they associate with elegance: hospitality, respect, good manners.

Arrogance attracts hatred and envy. Elegance arouses respect and Love.

Arrogance causes us to humiliate our fellow man or woman. Elegance teaches us to walk in the light.

Arrogance complicates words, because it believes that intelligence is only for the chosen few. Elegance transforms complex thoughts into something that everyone can understand.

When we are walking our chosen path, we walk elegantly, emanating light. Our steps are firm, our gaze keen, our movements beautiful. And even at the most difficult moments our adversaries can see no signs of weakness, because our elegance protects us.

Elegance is accepted and admired because it makes no effort to be elegant.

Only Love gives form to what, once, we could not even dream of.

And only elegance allows that form to be made manifest.

And a man who always woke up early to take his flocks to the pastures around the city said:

'You have studied in order to be able to speak these beautiful words, but we have to work to support our families.'

And he answered:

*   *   *

Beautiful words are spoken by poets. And one day, someone will write:

> *I fell asleep and dreamed that life was only*
>   *Happiness.*
> *I woke and discovered that life was*
>   *Duty.*
> *I did my Duty and discovered that life was*
>   *Happiness.*

Work is the manifestation of Love that binds people together. Through it, we discover that we are incapable of living without other people and that they need us just as much.

There are two types of work.

The first is the work we do because we have to in order to earn our daily bread. In that case, people are merely selling their time, not realising that they can never buy it back.

They spend their entire existence dreaming of the day when they can finally rest. When that day comes, they will be too old to enjoy everything life has to offer. Such people never take responsibility for their actions. They say: 'I have no choice.'

However, there is another type of work, which people also do in order to earn their daily bread but in which they try to fill each minute with dedication and love for others.

This second type of work we call the Offering.

For example, two people might be cooking the same meal and using exactly the same ingredients, but one is pouring Love into what he does and the other is merely trying to fill his belly. The result will be completely different, even though Love is not something that can be seen or weighed.

The person making the Offering is always rewarded. The more he shares out his affection, the more his affection grows.

When the Divine Energy set the Universe in motion, all the planets and stars, all the seas and forests, all the valleys and mountains were given the chance to take part in the Creation. And the same thing happened with mankind.

Some said: 'No, we don't want to. We won't be able to right wrongs or punish injustice.'

Others said: 'With the sweat of my brow I will water the fields, and that will be my way of praising the Creator.'

Then the devil came and whispered in his honeyed tones: 'You will have to carry that rock up to the top of the hill, and when you get there it will roll back down again to the bottom.'

And all those who believed in the devil said: 'The only meaning in life is to repeat the same task over and over.'

And those who did not believe in the devil answered: 'Then I will love the rock that I have to carry to the top of the mountain. That way, each minute by its side will be a minute spent closer to the one I love.'

The Offering is a wordless prayer. And like all prayers, it requires discipline – not the discipline of slavery, but of free choice.

There is no point in saying: 'Fate was unfair to me. While others are following their dreams, here I am just doing my job and earning my living.'

Fate is never unfair to anyone. We are all free to love or hate what we do.

When we love, we find the same joy in our daily activity as do those who one day set off in search of their dreams.

No one can know the importance or greatness of what they do. Therein lies the mystery and the beauty of the Offering: it is the mission that was entrusted to us, and we, in turn, need to trust it.

The labourer can plant, but he can't say to the sun: 'Shine more brightly this morning.' He can't say to the clouds: 'Make it rain this evening.' He has to do what is necessary: plough the field, sow the seeds and learn the gift of patience through contemplation.

He will experience moments of despair, when he sees his harvest ruined and feels that all his work was in vain. The person who has set off in search of his dreams will also have moments when he regrets his decision, and then all he wants is to go back and find a job that will pay him enough to survive.

The following day, though, the heart of every worker or every adventurer will once again be filled with euphoria and confidence. Both will see the fruits of the Offering and will be glad. Because both are singing the same song: the song of joy in the task that was entrusted to them.

The poet would die of hunger if there were no shepherds. The shepherd would die of sadness if he could not sing the words of the poet.

Through the Offering you are allowing others to love you. And you are teaching others to love through what you offer them.

And the same man who had asked about
work asked another question:

'Why are some people luckier
than others?'

And he answered:

*   *   *

Success does not come from having one's work recognised by others. It is the fruit of a seed that you lovingly planted.

When harvest time arrives, you can say to yourself: 'I succeeded.'

You succeeded in gaining respect for your work because you did not work only to survive, but to demonstrate your love for others.

You managed to finish what you began, even though you did not foresee all the traps along the way. And when your enthusiasm waned because of the difficulties you encountered, you reached for discipline. And when discipline seemed about to disappear because you were tired, you used your moments of repose to think about what steps you needed to take in the future.

You were not paralysed by the defeats that are inevitable in the lives of those who take risks. You didn't sit agonising over what you lost when you had an idea that didn't work.

You didn't stop when you experienced moments of glory, because you had not yet reached your goal.

And when you realised that you would have to ask for help, you did not feel humiliated. And when you learned that someone needed help, you showed them all that you had learned without fearing that you might be revealing secrets or were being used by others.

To him who knocks, the door will open.

He who asks will receive.

He who consoles knows that he will be consoled.

Even if none of these things happens when you are expecting it to, sooner or later you will see the fruits of the thing you shared with such generosity.

Success comes to those who do not waste time comparing what they are doing with what others are doing; it enters the house of the person who says 'I will do my best' every day.

People who seek only success rarely find it, because success is not an end in itself, but a consequence.

Obsession doesn't help at all; it only confuses us as to which path to follow and ends up taking away the pleasure of living.

Not everyone who owns a pile of gold the size of that hill to the south of our city is rich. The truly rich person is the one who is in contact with the energy of Love every second of his existence.

You must always have a goal in mind, but, as you go along, it costs nothing to stop now and then to enjoy the view around you. As you advance, step by step, you can see a little further into the distance, and take the opportunity to discover things you hadn't even noticed before.

At such moments, it is important to ask yourself: 'Are my values still intact? Am I trying to please others and do what they expect of me, or am I really convinced that my work is a manifestation of my soul and my enthusiasm? Do I want success at any price or do I want to be a successful person because I manage to fill my days with Love?'

Because that is what real success means: enriching your life, not cramming your coffers with gold.

A man might say: 'I will use my money to sow, plant, harvest and fill my granary with grain, so that I will lack for nothing.' But when the Unwanted Visitor arrives, all the man's efforts will have been in vain.

He that has ears to hear, let him hear.

Do not try to make the road shorter, but travel it in such a way that every action leaves the land more fertile and the landscape more beautiful.

Do not try to be the Master of Time. If you pick the fruit you planted too early, it will be green and give pleasure to no one. If, out of fear or insecurity, you decide to put off the moment of making the Offering, the fruit will have rotted.

Therefore, respect the time between sowing and harvesting.

Await the miracle of the transformation.

Until the wheat is in the oven, it cannot be called bread.

Until the words are spoken, they cannot be called a poem.

Until the threads are woven together by the hands of the person working them, they cannot be called cloth.

*   *   *

When the moment comes to show others your Offering, they will be amazed and will say to each other: 'There is a successful man, because everyone wants the fruits of his labours.'

No one will ask what it cost to produce those fruits, because anyone who does his work with love fills his creation with such intensity that it cannot be perceived by the eyes. Just as an acrobat flies easily through the air, with no apparent effort, success, when it comes, seems the most natural thing in the world.

Meanwhile, if anyone did dare to ask, the answer would be: I considered giving up, I thought God was no longer listening to me, I often had to change direction, and on other occasions I lost my way. Despite everything, though, I found it again and carried on, because I was convinced there was no other way to live my life.

I learned which bridges should be crossed and which should be burned.

*   *   *

I am poet, farmer, artist, soldier, father, trader, seller, teacher, politician, sage and someone who merely takes care of home and children.

I am aware that there are many people more famous than me and, often, that fame is richly deserved. In other cases, it is merely a manifestation of vanity or ambition, and will not stand the test of time.

What is success?

It is being able to go to bed each night with your soul at peace.

And Almira, who still believed that an
army of angels and archangels would
descend from the heavens to protect
the sacred city, said:

'Talk to us about miracles.'

And he answered:

*   *   *

What is a miracle?

We can define it in various ways: as something that goes against the laws of nature; an intercession in moments of deep crisis; healings and visions; impossible encounters; or as a last-minute intervention when the Unwanted Visitor arrives.

All these definitions are true, but a miracle goes beyond even that: it's something that suddenly fills our hearts with Love. When that happens, we feel a profound reverence for the grace God has bestowed on us.

Give us this day, Lord, our daily miracle.

Even if we are incapable of noticing it, because our mind is focused on great deeds and conquests. Even if we are too preoccupied with day-to-day life to know that our path was changed by it.

And when we are sad, help us to keep our eyes open to the life around us: a flower opening, the stars in the sky, the distant singing of a bird or a child's voice nearby.

Help us to understand that there are certain things so important that we have to discover them without anyone's help, and that we should not feel alone and helpless, because You are there with us, ready to intervene if our feet go perilously close to the abyss.

Help us to continue onward despite the fear, and to accept the inexplicable despite our need to explain and know everything.

Help us to understand that Love's strength lies in its contradictions, and that Love lasts because it changes and not because it stays the same and never faces any challenges.

And to understand, too, that each time we see the humble exalted and the arrogant humbled, we are witnessing a miracle.

Help us to know that when our legs are tired we can keep walking thanks to the strength in our hearts, and that when our hearts are tired we can still carry on thanks to the strength of our Faith.

Help us to see in each grain of desert sand proof of the miracle of difference, and may that encourage us to accept ourselves as we are. Because just as no two grains of sand are alike, so no two human beings will think and act in the same way.

Help us to be humble when we receive and joyful when we give.

Help us to understand that wisdom lies not in the answers we are given, but in the mystery of the questions that enrich our lives.

Help us never to be imprisoned by the things we think we know, because we know so little about Fate, and may this lead us to behave impeccably, making use of the four cardinal virtues: boldness, elegance, love and friendship.

* * *

Give us this day, Lord, our daily miracle.

Just as there are many paths to the top of a mountain, so there are many paths to achieving our goal. Help us to recognise the only one that is worth following, the one on which Love is to be found.

Help us to awaken the Love sleeping within us before we awaken love in other people. Only then will we be able to attract affection, enthusiasm and respect.

Help us to distinguish between battles that are ours, battles into which we are propelled against our will, and battles that we cannot avoid because Fate has placed them in our path.

May our eyes open so that we can see that no two days are ever the same. Each one brings with it a different miracle, which allows us to go on breathing, dreaming and walking in the sun.

May our ears also open to hear the very apposite words that suddenly emerge from the mouth of one of our fellows, even though we haven't asked for his advice and he has no idea what is going on in our soul at that moment.

And when we open our mouth, may we speak not just the language of men, but the language of angels too, saying: 'Miracles do not go against the laws of nature; we only think that because we do not know nature's laws.'

And when we achieve this, may we bow our head in respect and say: 'I was blind, but now I can see. I was dumb, but now I can speak. I was deaf, but now I can hear. Because God worked his miracle within me, and everything I thought was lost has been restored.'

*   *   *

Miracles tear away the veils and change everything, but do not let us see what lies behind the veils.

They allow us to escape unharmed from the valley of the shadow of death, but do not tell us which road led us to the mountains of joy and light.

They open doors that were locked with impossible padlocks, but they use no key.

They surround the suns with planets so that they do not feel alone in the Universe, and they keep the planets from getting too close so that they won't be devoured by the suns.

They transform the wheat into bread through work, the grape into wine through patience, and death into life through the resurrection of dreams.

Therefore, Lord, give us this day our daily miracle.

And forgive us if we are not always capable of recognising it.

And a man who was listening to the war
chants coming from beyond the city
walls and who feared for his
family, said:

'Speak to us about anxiety.'

And he answered:

*   *   *

There is nothing wrong with anxiety.

Although we cannot control God's time, it is part of the human condition to want to receive the thing we are waiting for as quickly as possible.

Or to drive away whatever is causing our fear.

This is so from childhood onwards, until we reach the age when we become indifferent to life. Because as long as we are intensely connected to the present moment, we will always be waiting anxiously for someone or something.

How can you tell a passionate heart to be still and to contemplate the miracles of Creation in silence, free of tension, fear and unanswerable questions?

Anxiety is part of love, and should not be blamed because of that.

How can you tell someone not to worry when he has invested his money and his life in a dream but has yet to see any results? The farmer cannot speed the progress of the seasons in order to pick the fruit he planted, but he waits impatiently for the coming of autumn and harvest-time.

How can you ask a warrior not to feel anxious before a battle?

He has trained to the point of exhaustion for this moment, he has given of his best, and although he believes he is prepared he fears that all his efforts could prove to be in vain.

Anxiety was born in the very same moment as mankind. And since we will never be able to master it, we will have to learn to live with it – just as we have learned to live with storms.

*   *   *

For those who cannot learn to do so, life will be a nightmare.

The very thing they should be grateful for – all the hours that make up a day – becomes a curse. They want time to pass more quickly, not realising that this will also hasten their encounter with the Unwanted Visitor.

Even worse, in an attempt to drive away anxiety, they do things that make them even more anxious.

The mother, waiting for her son to come home, begins to imagine the worst.

The lover thinks: 'My beloved is mine and I am his. And in the broad ways I sought him, but I found him not.' With every corner I pass and with each person I ask and who fails to answer my questions, I allow the normal anxiety of love to be transformed into despair.

The worker, while he awaits the fruits of his labours, tries to occupy himself with other tasks, each of which will bring him more moments of waiting. It will not be long before each single anxiety has combined to become one larger anxiety, and he can no longer see the sky or the stars or his children playing.

And mother, lover and worker alike all cease living their lives and simply expect the worst; they listen to rumours and complain that the day seems never-ending. They become aggressive with friends, family and employees. They eat badly, either consuming too much or unable to keep anything down. And at night, they lay their head on the pillow but cannot sleep.

That is when anxiety weaves a veil through which only the eyes of the soul can see.

And the eyes of the soul are bleary with tiredness.

At that point, in walks one of humankind's worst enemies: obsession.

Obsession arrives and says:

'Your fate now belongs to me. I will make you look for things that do not exist.

'Your joy in living belongs to me too. From now on, your heart will know no peace, because I will drive out enthusiasm and take its place.

'I will allow fear to spread throughout the world, and you will always feel afraid, but without knowing why. You don't need to know, you just need to stay afraid and thus feed and fatten your fear.

'Your work, which was once an Offering, has also been taken over by me. The others will say that you set a fine example, because you drive yourself so hard, and you will smile and thank them for the compliment.

'But in your heart, I will be saying that your work is now mine, and I will use it to distance you from everything and everyone – from your friends, from your son, from yourself.

'Work harder, so you won't have to think. Work harder than you need to, so that you can stop living altogether.

'Your Love, which was once a manifestation of the Divine Energy, belongs to me too. And the person you love will be unable to leave your side for a moment, because I am there in your heart saying: "Careful, she might go away and never come back."

'Your son, who once would have followed his own path in the world, will now be mine as well. I will have you surround him with unnecessary worries that destroy his taste for adventure and risk, that make him suffer whenever he displeases you and that leave him feeling guilty because he has failed to live up to your expectations.'

* * *

Therefore, although anxiety is part of life, never let it control you.

If it comes too close, say: 'I'm not worried about tomorrow, because God is there already, waiting for me.'

If it tries to persuade you that taking on lots of jobs means having a productive life, say: 'I need time to look at the stars in order to feel inspired and to be able to do my job well.'

If it threatens you with the ghost of hunger, say: 'Man does not live by bread alone, but by every word that proceeds out of the mouth of God.'

If it tells you that your beloved might not come back, say: 'My beloved is mine and I am hers. She is grazing her flocks by the river, and I can hear her singing, even from afar. When she returns home, she will be tired and happy, and I will make her some food and watch over her sleep.'

If it tells you that your son has no respect for the love you lavished on him, answer: 'Excessive caution destroys the soul and the heart, because living is an act of courage, and an act of courage is always an act of love.'

That way you will keep anxiety at bay.

It will never disappear, but the great wisdom of life is to realise that we can be the masters of the things that try to enslave us.

And a young man said:

'Tell us what the future holds.'

And he answered:

*   *   *

We all know what awaits us in the future:
the Unwanted Visitor, who could arrive at any
hour, without warning, and say: 'Come with
me.'

And however much we may not want to, we
will have no choice. At that moment, our greatest joy, or perhaps our greatest sadness, will be
to look back at the past and answer the question:
'Did I give enough love?'

We must love. I am not speaking only of love
for another person. Loving means being open to
miracles, to victories and defeats, to everything

that happens each day that is given us to walk upon the face of the Earth.

Our soul is governed by four invisible forces: love, death, power and time.

We must love because we are loved by God.

We must be aware of the Unwanted Visitor if we are fully to understand life.

We must struggle in order to grow, but without becoming trapped by whatever power we might gain from that. We know that such power is worthless.

Finally, we must accept that our soul, although eternal, is, at this moment, caught in the web of time, with all its possibilities and limitations.

Our dream, the desire that is in our soul, did not come out of nowhere. Someone placed it there. And that Someone, who is pure Love and wants only our happiness, did so only because he also gave us the tools to realise our dreams and our desires.

When you are going through difficult times, remember: you may have lost some major battles, but you survived and you're still here.

That is a victory. Show your happiness and celebrate your ability to go forward.

Manuscript found in Accra 155

Pour your love generously out onto the fields and pastures, down the streets of the big city and across the dunes of the desert.

Show that you care about the poor, for they are an opportunity for you to display the virtue of charity.

And care, too, about the rich who distrust everything and everyone, keeping their granaries crammed with grain and their coffers full, but who, despite all that, cannot drive away loneliness.

Never miss an opportunity to show your love, especially to those close to you, because we are always at our most cautious with them for fear of being hurt.

Love – because you will be the first to benefit. The world around you will reward you, even if, at first, you say to yourself: 'They don't understand my love.'

Love does not need to be understood. It needs only to be shown.

Therefore, what the future holds for you depends entirely on your capacity for love.

And for that, you must have absolute and total confidence in what you are doing. Don't let others say: 'That road is better,' or 'That route is easier.'

The greatest gift God gave us is the power to make decisions.

We were all told, from childhood on, that what we wanted to do was impossible. As we accumulate years, we also accumulate the sand of prejudices, fears and guilt.

Free yourself from that. Not tomorrow, not tonight, but now.

As I said: many of us believe that we will hurt those we love if we leave everything behind in the name of our dreams.

But those who truly want the best for us want us to be happy, even if they can't understand what we are doing and even if, at first, they try to stop us going ahead by means of threats, promises and tears.

The adventure of the days to come needs to be filled with romance, because the world needs that; therefore, when you are mounted on your horse, feel the wind on your face and enjoy the sense of freedom.

But don't forget that you have a long journey ahead. If you surrender totally to the romance of

it all, you might fall. If you don't stop occasionally to let both you and your horse rest, your
horse might die of thirst or exhaustion.

Listen to the wind, but don't forget about
your horse.

And precisely when everything seems to be
going well and your dream is almost within
your grasp, that is when you must be more alert
than ever. Because when your dream is almost
within your grasp, you will be assailed by terrible guilt.

You will see that you are about to arrive at a
place where very few have ever set foot, and
you will think that you don't deserve what life
is giving you.

You will forget all the obstacles you over-
came, all that you suffered and sacrificed. And
because of that feeling of guilt, you could uncon-
sciously destroy everything that took you so
long to build.

That is the most dangerous of obstacles,
because renouncing victory has about it a certain
aura of sanctity.

But if a man understands that he is worthy of
what he has struggled so long for, he will realise

that he did not get there alone and must respect the Hand that led him.

Only someone capable of honouring each step he takes can comprehend his own worth.

And a man who knew how to write and who was frantically trying to note down every word that the Copt said, paused to rest, feeling as if he were in a kind of trance. The square, the weary faces, the religious men who were listening in silence all seemed part of a dream.

And in order to prove to himself that what he was experiencing was real, he said:

'Speak to us about loyalty.'

And he answered:

*   *   *

Loyalty can be compared to a shop selling exqui-
sitely decorated vases, a shop to which Love has
given us the key.

Each of those vases is beautiful because it is
different, as is every person, every drop of rain,
every rock sleeping on the mountainside.

Sometimes, due to age or some unsuspected
defect, a shelf collapses and falls. And the shop-
owner says to himself: 'I invested years of my
time and my love on this collection, but the
vases have betrayed me and broken.'

The man sells his shop and leaves. He becomes a solitary, embittered individual, believing that he will never trust anyone again.

It's true that some vases do break – a promise of loyalty broken. In that case, it's best to sweep up the pieces and throw them away, because what was broken will never be the same again.

But sometimes the reasons why a shelf collapses and falls go beyond mere human intentions: it could be an earthquake, an enemy invasion, or clumsiness on the part of someone who enters the shop without looking where he is going.

Men and women blame each other for the disaster. They say: 'Someone should have foreseen what was going to happen.' Or: 'If I had been in charge, these problems could have been avoided.'

Nothing could be further from the truth. We are all prisoners of the sands of time, and we have no control over them.

Time passes and the shelf that fell gets mended.

Other vases fighting for their place in the world are put there. The new shop-owner, who understands that nothing lasts, smiles and says to himself: 'That tragedy opened up an opportunity for me and I will try to make the most of it. I will discover works of art I never even knew existed.'

The beauty of a shop selling decorated vases is that each vase is unique, but, when they are placed side by side, the vases exude harmony and reflect the hard work of the potter and the art of the painter.

Each work of art could easily say: 'I want to be noticed and I'm going to get out of here.' But the moment it tries to do that, it will be transformed into a pile of broken shards, with no value.

And as it is with vases, so it is with men and women.

And so it is with tribes and ships and trees and stars.

Once we understand this, we can sit next to our neighbour at the end of the day and listen with respect to what he has to say and say what he needs to hear. And neither of us will try to impose our ideas on the other.

Beyond the mountains that separate the tribes, beyond the distance that separates bodies, there exists the community of spirits. We are part of that community, where there are no streets peopled with pointless words, only broad avenues that connect what is distant and sometimes have to be repaired because of the damage caused by time.

Thus, the returning lover will never be eyed with distrust, because loyalty accompanies his every step.

And the man who, yesterday, was seen as an enemy because there was a war being waged, will now be seen as a friend, because the war is over and life goes on.

The son who left will eventually return, and he will return rich in the experiences he had along the way. His father will receive him with open arms and say to his servants: 'Bring the best robe for him and put a ring on his finger and sandals on his feet; because my son was dead and is alive again. He was lost and is found.'

And a man, whose brow was marked by time and whose body was marked by scars that told the story of the battles in which he had fought, said:

'Speak to us of the weapons we must use when all is lost.'

And he answered:

* * *

Where there is loyalty, weapons are of no use.

All weapons are instruments of evil because they are not the instruments of the wise man.

Loyalty has its roots in respect and respect is the fruit of Love, and Love drives out the demons of the imagination – which distrust everything and everyone – and, instead, returns purity to our gaze.

When a wise man wants to make someone weak, he first makes that person believe that he is strong. The other man will then fall into the trap of challenging someone even stronger and be destroyed.

When a wise man wants to bring someone low, he first makes that person climb the highest mountain in the world to allow him the illusion that he is very powerful. The other man will then believe that he can go still higher and plunge into the abyss.

When a wise man covets something that belongs to another man, he loads him with gifts. The other man will have so many useless objects to take care of that he will lose everything else, because he is too busy trying to keep what he thinks he owns.

When a wise man cannot discover what his opponent is planning, he feigns an attack. We are always prepared to defend ourselves, because we all live with the fear and paranoia that other people don't like us.

His opponent – however brilliant he may be – is insecure and reacts with excessive violence to the provocation. In doing so, he reveals what weapons he has, and the wise man thus discovers what his opponent's strong and weak points are. Then, knowing exactly what kind of reaction to expect, the wise man either attacks or retreats.

This is how those who appear submissive and weak conquer and defeat those who are powerful and strong.

*   *   *

And so wise men often defeat warriors, but warriors also defeat wise men. To avoid this, it is best to seek the peace and repose that exists in the differences between human beings.

The wounded person should ask himself: 'Is it worth filling my heart with hatred and dragging the weight of it around with me?'

He is thus making use of one of Love's qualities – namely Forgiveness. This helps him to rise above all the insults spoken in the heat of battle, insults that time will soon erase, just as the wind erases footsteps from the sands of the desert.

When you forgive, the person who insulted you feels humbled in his error and becomes loyal.

Let us, therefore, be aware of the forces that move us.

The true hero is not the man who was born for great deeds, but the one who has managed to build a shield of loyalty around him out of many small things.

Thus, when he saves his adversary from certain death or from betrayal, his gesture will never be forgotten.

The true lover is not the one who says: 'You need to be by my side and I need to take care of you, because we are loyal to one another,' but the one who realises that loyalty must go hand-in-hand with freedom. And without fear of betrayal, he accepts and respects the other person's dream, trusting in the greater power of Love.

The true friend is not the one who says: 'You wounded me today, and I am sad.'

He says: 'You wounded me today for reasons unknown to me and possibly to you as well, but tomorrow I know that I will be able to count on your help. And so I will not be sad.'

And the friend responds: 'You are a loyal friend, because you said what you felt. There is nothing worse than a friend who confuses loyalty with accepting our every fault.'

The most destructive of weapons is not the spear or the siege cannon, which can wound a body and demolish a wall. The most terrible of all weapons is the word, which can ruin a life without leaving a trace of blood, and whose wounds never heal.

Let us, then, be the masters of our tongue and not the slaves of our words. Even if words are used against us, let us not enter a battle that cannot be won. The moment we place ourselves on the same level as some vile adversary, we will be fighting in the dark, and the only winner will be the Lord of Darkness.

*   *   *

Loyalty is a pearl among grains of sand, and only those who really understand its meaning can see it.

Thus the Sower of Discord can pass the same spot a thousand times and never see the little jewel that keeps those who need to remain united together.

Loyalty can never be imposed by force, fear, insecurity or intimidation.

It is a choice that only strong spirits have the courage to make.

And because it is a choice, it will never tolerate betrayal, but will always be generous with mistakes.

And because it is a choice, it withstands time and passing conflicts.

And one of the young men in the audience, seeing that the sun was almost below the horizon and that soon this encounter with the Copt would come to an end, asked:

'And what about enemies?'

And he answered:

*   *   *

The truly wise do not grieve over the living or the dead. Therefore, accept the battle that awaits you tomorrow, because we are made of the Eternal Spirit, which often places us in situations that we need to confront.

At such moments, set aside all futile questions, because they merely slow down the warrior's reflexes.

A warrior on the battlefield is fulfilling his destiny, and he must surrender himself to that. Pity those who think they must kill or die! The Divine Energy cannot be destroyed; it simply changes its form. The wise men of Antiquity said:

> '*Accept this as part of some superior plan and go forward. Man is not defined by earthly battles, because just as the wind changes direction, so do luck and victory. Today's loser will be tomorrow's winner, but in order for that to happen, combat must be embraced with honour.*
>
> '*Just as someone puts on new clothes, discarding the old, so the soul accepts new material bodies, abandoning the old and the useless. Knowing this, you must not suffer because of the body.*'

That is the combat we will face tonight or tomorrow morning. History will record what happens.

But since we are reaching the end of our meeting, we cannot waste time on that.

I wish, therefore, to speak of other enemies: those we find beside us.

We will all have to face many adversaries in our lives, but the most difficult to defeat will be the ones we fear.

We will always meet rivals in everything we do, but the most dangerous are those we believe to be our friends.

We all suffer when our dignity is attacked or wounded, but the greatest pain will be caused by those we thought were examples to be followed.

None of us can avoid meeting those who will betray and slander us, but we can drive away the evil before it shows its true face. Any excessively kind behaviour could betray a knife hidden behind the back and ready to be used.

Loyal men and women do not bother to show what they are like, because other loyal spirits understand their qualities and defects.

Beware of anyone who tries to please you all the time.

And beware of the pain you can cause yourself by allowing a vile and cowardly heart to be part of your world. Once the evil has been done, there is no point in blaming anyone: it was the owner of the house who opened the door.

The more fragile the slanderer, the more dangerous his actions. Do not make yourself vulnerable to those weak spirits who cannot bear to encounter a strong spirit.

If someone confronts you over ideas or ideals, step up and accept the fight, because conflict is present in every moment of our lives and sometimes it needs to show itself in the broad light of day.

But do not fight in order to prove that you are right or to impose your ideas or ideals on someone else. Only accept the fight as a way of keeping your spirit clean and your will spotless. When the fight is over, both sides will emerge as winners, because they tested their limitations and their abilities.

Even if, at first, one of them says 'I won' and the other grows sad, thinking 'I lost'.

Since both respect the courage and determination of the other, the time will come when they will once again walk along hand-in-hand, even if they have to wait a thousand years for that to happen.

Meanwhile, if someone merely wishes to provoke you, shake the dust from your feet and carry on. Only fight with a worthy opponent, not with someone who uses trickery to prolong a war that is already over, as does sometimes happen.

Such cruelty does not come from the warriors who meet on the battlefield and know why they are there, but from those who manipulate victory and defeat for their own ends.

The enemy is not the person standing before you, sword in hand. It is the person standing next to you with a dagger concealed behind his back.

The most important of wars is not waged with a lofty spirit and a soul accepting of its fate. It is the war that is going on now as we are speaking and whose battlefield is the Spirit, where Good and Evil, Courage and Cowardice, Love and Fear face each other.

Never repay hatred with hatred, but with justice.

The world does not divide up into enemies and friends, but into the weak and the strong.

The strong are generous in victory.

The weak gang up on the losers, unaware that defeat is only a transitory thing. From among the losers, they choose those who seem most vulnerable.

If the same were to happen to you, ask yourself if you would like to take on the role of victim.

If the answer is 'Yes', you will never be free of that choice for the rest of your life. And you will be easy prey whenever you are faced by a decision that demands courage. You might talk like a winner, but the look of defeat in your eyes will always be there, and everyone will notice.

If the answer is 'No', stand your ground. It is better to rebel while your wounds are easily treated – even if it takes time and patience.

You will spend a few sleepless nights, thinking: 'I don't deserve this.'

Or thinking what an unfair world it is because it failed to give you the welcome you were expecting, or feeling ashamed at the humiliation endured in front of your colleagues, your lover or your parents.

But, if you hold fast, the pack of hyenas will eventually move off and go in search of someone else to play the role of victim. They will have to learn the same lesson for themselves, because no one else will be able to help them.

*   *   *

Therefore, your enemies are not the adversaries who were put there to test your courage. They are the cowards who were put there to test your weakness.

Night had fallen now. The Copt turned
to the religious men who had been
listening to all that he had said and
asked them if they had anything to add.
All three nodded.

And the rabbi said:

*   *   *

When a great rabbi saw that the Jews were being mistreated, he went into the forest, lit a sacred fire and said a special prayer asking God to protect his people. And God sent him a miracle.

Later, his disciple went into the same part of the forest and said: 'Master of the Universe, I do not know how to light the sacred fire, but I do know the special prayer; please, hear me!' And the miracle happened again.

A generation passed, and another rabbi, seeing how his people were being persecuted, went into the forest and said: 'I do not know how to light the sacred fire, nor do I know the special prayer, but I still remember the place. Help us, O Lord!' And the Lord helped them.

Fifty years later, another rabbi, who was crippled, spoke to God, saying: 'I do not know how to light the sacred fire, nor do I know the special prayer, and I can't even find the place in the forest. All I can do is tell this story and hope that God will hear me.'

And again the miracle occurred.

Go forth, then, and tell the story of this evening.

*   *   *

And the imam who was in charge of the Al-Aqsa Mosque waited respectfully for his friend the rabbi to finish speaking, then said:

*   *   *

A man knocked on the door of a Bedouin friend's house to ask him a favour:

'Will you lend me four thousand dinars to pay off a debt?'

His friend asked his wife to gather together everything they had of value, but it still wasn't enough. They had to go out and beg money from their neighbours until they had the necessary amount.

When the man left, the wife noticed that her husband was crying.

'Why are you sad? Now that we are in debt to our neighbours, are you afraid that we won't be able to repay it?'

'No, it's not that. I'm crying because he is a dearly beloved friend, and yet I knew nothing of the difficulties he was in. I only found out when he came and knocked on my door and asked to borrow some money.'

Go forth, therefore, and tell everyone what you heard this evening, so that we can help our brother before he needs us to.

And when the imam finished speaking, the Christian priest began:

*   *   *

A sower went out to sow. And it came to pass that as he sowed, some seed fell by the wayside, and the birds of the air came and devoured it. And some fell on stony ground, where it had not much earth; and immediately it sprang up, because it had no depth of earth. But when the sun was up, it became scorched, and because it had no root, it withered away. And some fell among thorns, and the thorns grew up and choked it, and it yielded no fruit. And some that fell on good ground did yield fruit that sprang up and increased; and brought forth, some thirty, and some sixty, some a hundred-fold.

Therefore, scatter your seed wherever you go, because we can never know which seeds will grow and flourish and enlighten the next generation.

Night now covered the city of Jerusalem, and the Copt asked everyone to return to their houses and record everything they had heard, and for those who did not know how to write to try and remember his words. However, before the multitude left, he said:

'Do not think that I am come to spread peace upon the Earth. No, from this night on, we will travel the world bearing an invisible sword, so that we can fight the demons of intolerance and lack of understanding. Try to carry that sword as far as your legs will take you. And when your legs can take you no further, pass on the word or the manuscript, always choosing people worthy of wielding that sword.

'If a village or a city refuses to welcome you, do not insist. Walk back along the path by which you came and shake the dust from your feet. For they will be condemned to repeat the same mistakes for many generations.

'Blessed are those who hear these words or read this manuscript, because the veil will be rent from top to bottom, and there is nothing hidden that will not be revealed to you.

'Go in peace.'

Life is a
journey

Make sure you don't miss a thing.
Live it with Paulo Coelho.

Visit **f** /paulocoelho

How can you find your heart's desire?

A world-wide phenomenon; an inspiration for anyone seeking their path in life.

The Alchemist

How do we see the amazing in the everyday

When two young lovers are reunited, they discover anew the truth of what lies in their hearts.

By the River Piedra I Sat Down & Wept

What are you searching for?

A transforming journey on the pilgrims' road to Santiago – and the first of Paulo's extraordinary books.

The Pilgrimage

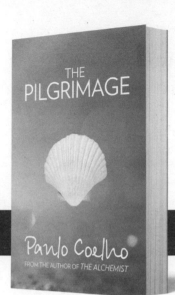

Can faith triumph over suffering?

Paulo Coelho's brilliant telling of the story of Elijah, who was forced to choose between love and duty.

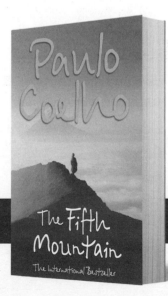

The Fifth Mountain

Is life always worth living?

A fundamental moral question explored as only Paulo Coelho can.

Veronika Decides to Die

Could you be tempted into evil?

The inhabitants of a small town are challenged by a mysterious stranger to choose between good and evil.

The Devil & Miss Prym

Are you brave enough to live your dream?

Strategies and inspiration to help you follow your own path in a troubled world.

Manual of the Warrior of Light

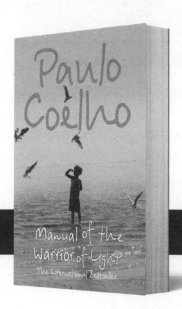

Can sex be sacred?

An unflinching exploration of the lengths we go to in our search for love, sex and spirituality.

Eleven Minutes

How far would you go for your obsession?

A sweeping story of love, loss and longing that spans the world.

The Zahir

What does it mean to be truly alive?

Powerful tales of living and dying, destiny and choice, and love lost and found.

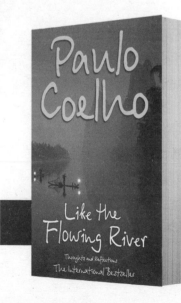

Like the Flowing River

Can we dare to be true to ourselves?

A story that will transform the way we think about love, joy and sacrifice.

The Witch of Portobello

How will you know who your soulmate is?

A moving tale of passion, mystery and spirituality.

Brida

What happens when obsession turns to murder?

An enthralling story of jealousy, death and suspense.

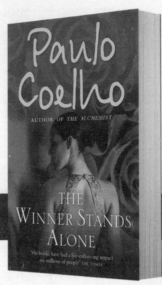

Are you where you want to be?

Read *Aleph*. And rewrite your life.

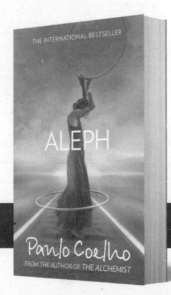